CHELTENH

Cheltenham Festivals is the charitable organisation wh[illegible] internationally acclaimed Jazz, Science, Music and Literature Festivals. Through cutting-edge and creative programming, Cheltenham's four inspirational festivals have been at the forefront of the UK's cultural scene since the inaugural Music Festival in 1945.

By championing the best up-and-coming young talent, celebrating the work of established artists and commissioning unique and surprising performances, Cheltenham Festivals enriches the cultural lives of its audiences. Schools, young people and our local community can enjoy the Festivals year round through our extensive programme of educational workshops, talks, projects and inspiring activities.

For more information and details of how to support Cheltenham Festivals, see www.cheltenhamfestivals.com.

FIRST STORY

First Story changes lives through writing.

We believe that writing can transform lives, and that there is dignity and power in every young person's story.

First Story brings talented, professional writers into secondary schools serving low-income communities to work with teachers and students to foster creativity and communication skills. By helping students find their voices through intensive, fun programmes, First Story raises aspirations and gives students the skills and confidence to achieve them.

For more information and details of how to support First Story, see www.firststory.org.uk or contact us at info@firststory.org.uk.

Inside Our Heads
ISBN 978-0-85748-169-6

Published in Great Britain by
First Story Limited · Sixth Floor · 2 Seething Lane
London EC3N 4AT
www.firststory.org.uk
in partnership with
Cheltenham Festivals · 109–111 Bath Road
Cheltenham GL53 7LS
www.cheltenhamfestivals.com

Typesetter: Avon DataSet Ltd
Cover Illustration: E Barrett
Cover Designer: Adam Cohen
Printed in the UK by Intype Libra Ltd

Cheltenham Festivals is a registered charity number 251765.

First Story is a registered charity number 1122939 and a private company limited by guarantee incorporated in England with number 06487410. First Story is a business name of First Story Limited.

Inside Our Heads

An Anthology

By The Cheltenham Festivals First Story Group
At Gloucester Academy

Edited and introduced by Alicia Stubbersfield | 2015

CHELTENHAMFESTIVALS
FIRST STORY
Creativity Literacy Confidence

As Patron of First Story I am delighted that it continues to foster and inspire the creativity and talent of young people in challenging secondary schools.

I firmly believe that nurturing a passion for reading and writing is vital to the health of our country. I am therefore greatly encouraged to know that young people in this school – and across the country – have been meeting each week throughout the year in order to write together.

I send my warmest congratulations to everybody who is published in this anthology.

Camilla

HRH The Duchess of Cornwall

Thank You

The Hitchins Family Trust within the **Gloucestershire Community Foundation** and the **Wates Foundation**.

Melanie Curtis at **Avon DataSet** for her overwhelming support for Cheltenham Festivals First Story and for giving her time in typesetting this anthology.

The **University of Gloucestershire** illustration department for their support for Cheltenham Festivals First Story, and **E Barrett** in particular for giving their time to illustrate the cover of this anthology.

Adam Cohen for designing the cover of this anthology.

Intype Libra for printing this anthology at a discounted rate; **Tony Chapman** and **Moya Birchall** at Intype Libra for their advice.

The Wilson Cheltenham Art Gallery and Museum.

The Trustees of Cheltenham Festivals:
Peter Bond, Dominic Collier, Susan Blanchfield, Lewis Carnie, Oli Christie, Prof Russell Foster CBE, Edward Gillespie OBE, Prof Averil Macdonald, Baroness Gail Rebuck and Dr Diane Savory OBE.

The Advisory Group of The Times and The Sunday Times Cheltenham Literature Festivals:
Clare Alexander, Clare Clark, Geraldine Collinge, James Daunt, Allie Esiri, Jonny Geller, Andrew Holgate, Caroline Hutton, Dotti Irving, Laurel Ives, Annalena McAfee, Robbie Millen, Eleanor Mills, Gail Rebuck, Emma Tucker, Shami Chakrabarti.

HRH The Duchess of Cornwall, Patron of First Story.

Most importantly we would like to thank the students, teachers and writers who have worked so hard to make Cheltenham Festivals First Story a success this year, as well as the many individuals and organisations (including those we may have omitted to name) who have given their generous time, support and advice.

Contents

Introduction

Alicia Stubbersfield

Writer-in-Residence

Editing *Inside My Head* and reading the students' work again, I was struck by the thought and perception revealed in these pieces. The language is precise and muscular, the imagery is original and compelling, and the engaging content is often very moving.

It will be clear to any reader that these young people are thinking and working like writers. One of the great benefits of this Cheltenham Festivals and First Story collaboration with Gloucester Academy is that the sessions are not examination-focused. The sessions are about allowing the students to explore their own creativity, to 'be' writers and to value their writing for its own sake, not because it will gain a good mark. Having said that, many of the high-level skills required by the school were being developed through the work we did.

I introduced the students to work by writers as varied as Pablo Neruda, Carol Ann Duffy, Maura Dooley, Max Hastings, Michael Morpurgo and Vernon Scannell. We read their poems and prose and used them as models for writing. Each student took the ideas and very much made them their own. We spent an amazing afternoon in Cheltenham's Wilson Gallery where the students toured the gallery and then wrote from a bronze sculpture, 'The Broken Limber', by Robert Lindsey Clark. We read extracts about first world war conditions and discussed approaches to writing about the sculpture. Students were invited to write from any point of view, including the horse's (and there is a poem in the anthology from that point of view!), paying close attention to the five senses. The writing that came from this stimulus was extraordinarily thoughtful and detailed.

Paying attention – whether to the detailed use of the five senses, to finding exactly the right word or image, to the task, or to each other – has been our focus, and I am sure that anyone reading this anthology will be amazed by the writers' ability to do precisely that, conjuring scenes and emotions with real accuracy.

Of course a project like this is not just about the professional writer and the students. I have been extremely fortunate to work with a wonderful teacher, Katy Trivess, who is exceptionally well-organised and has that very rare quality, the ability to be both good fun with the students while also commanding their respect. My part in this would have been very much harder without her wholehearted participation.

It has been a real privilege to work with such a brilliant group of students.

Inside Some of Our Heads

Courtney Bullingham

Pictures of loved ones.
Letters from the bank for my parents,
birthday and Christmas cards,
teddy bears from childhood,
certificates from school,
medals from dance competitions.
Newspapers.
Tapes from the friends and family,
favourite books,
clothes I call fashionable,
lyrics to that song I'm going to write next.
Thinking: what am I to do with
this unwanted stuff?
Dust covering the shelves,
old instruments I don't play anymore.
Thinking: how am I going decorate your room?
Or where will I put the Christmas decs
and the Christmas tree now I've finished with them?
It's not impossible to have
lots of things in your head!

Louise Cronshaw

Warm soapy water
becoming colder by the second
not useful for much but mopping.

Compost ready so the roses can grow
water in the bowl below.
The roses are dying, thirsty for water.
No sun, no water, no food
A gorgeous flower gone to waste
until it is fed

My favourite rubber I've had for years,
pencil sharpenings scattered.
Blue and black pens with hardly any ink left in them.
£1 colouring pencils that are light and dull.

The fakery that I slap on my face,
bronzer broken and shattered,
mascara all over the brushes.
The brushes are hardly any use
more and more shoved in.

The education that can change my world,
books and papers crumpled up,
water leaking over my textbooks,
blazer all creased and shoved inside.

It has a surprise.
Could give me a big lovely grin.

Could not tickle my fancy.
The anxiety inside before I open the lid.

The refreshing taste of the water,
sweetness of squash,
fizz of Fanta.

Is it full of delicious treats or various spices?
Coriander and nutmeg drift up my nose
or the sweetness I can taste as I open the door
Maybe it's just bread and crumpets
or tins of baked beans and spaghetti hoops.

My favourite odd socks,
comfy and cosy,
worn only rarely.
A pattern of sheep
that reminds me of the countryside

My favourite black plain skater dress,
barely fitting me anymore,
just hangs there waiting to be worn.

Chloe Davis

Hundreds of vibrantly coloured pencils
under many more rainbow pens,
long, numbered rulers
detailed with measurements,
fat rubbery rubbers breaking
from being used too often.

Aaron Gomez

Sausages, sweet gooseberry jam on top of bread,
beautiful bananas, killers looking for blood,
robbers wanting more than they can afford,
gangs looking for a fight which ends up
with someone on the ground dead,
death, hearses, putrid bodies in the ground,
dirty, polluted cities people are scared to go inside.

Michal Hagner

Jam
pens, boring school books,
plain white paper
party shopping
silly children
wilted roses
soup
my slow phone, sweet wrappers
old stuff
dirty fish
ink and printed paper
smelly rubbish
stinky unwashed feet.

Humzah Jaffer

The creations of God,
the knowledge of power,
stolen money rattling.

Children's toys: Lego, match attacks,
Pokémon figures, loved treasures
which will never be forgotten.

Water with dead insects floating,
a rotten, stinking body
that used to be loved.

Bethany Hutton

A blurred body, refusing to leave
The comfortable warmth.

A decomposing corpse, slowly being eaten
by maggots, worms, and cockroaches.

Jam, peanut butter, apricot sweets, mouldy fused candy
and fresh chocolate biscuits.

Bright and vibrant flowers from a new love,
maybe some old rotten ones from the love before.

Different religions, races; bullies, weak links, friends and
enemies.

The greatest secrets known to man,
hats, coats and scrap paper which just appears out of nowhere.

Pocked and prodded animals wail, while children watch, scream,
laugh.

Murders, masterminds, and criminals, all cooped up like animals
in a cage.

Susan Jones

A turquoise ruler,
black biro,
dark, grey pencil,
rainbow of colouring pencils,
a chipped protractor,
a silver, pointed compass,
childhood toys;
Lady from *Lady and the Tramp*,
a tattered *Winnie the Pooh* bear,
moth-eaten baby clothes,
birthday cards from deceased relatives,
a discoloured medal,
freshly cut red roses,
enchanting pink tulips,
baby's breath that reminds me of past memories,
plastic bees that buzz through my mind
and laughter echoing…

Vikki Kirby

Blunt pencils,
scraggly old rubbers,
stolen pens,
and the colourful grit from sharpenings,

Powder everywhere,
Seven million lipglosses I don't wear,
Four different shades of foundation,
armies of makeup brushes,

nothing to put in them,
awaiting the present.
Who will get it?
Or will it be left unloved?

Old sore feet,
spun around in hammer so often,
school tights – boring –
making an outfit complete.

Full of carb and energy powder,
powdery water,
vile but slightly satisfying taste
helping me through training.

Clutter of clothes,
makeup scattered,
sweet packets,
and fairy lights.

Rainwater
making the garden bloom,
awaiting the storm,
helpful yet ugly.

Clothes I don't really need,
labels of unworn tops,
this one,
blue like the others but unworn.

Lunchboxes,
sacks of school letters from months ago,
pens that should be in my pencil case but aren't.
Lipbalms galore.

What a weird place.
Plans for the future,
but for now, full of stuff… just stuff, meaningless stuff.

Kyania May

White, freshly watered lilies that smell wonderful
and make me think I'm by the riverside.
Cheesy, unwashed feet needing
to be covered by socks.
Raw meat, fish fingers and other Iceland deals.
Bread, eggs, milk, butter, most of the everyday foods.
Hot chocolate warms up
my hands when I hold it
and smells milky and soft.
A cold, decomposed body wearing a neat suit.
Brutal criminals and the worst people I can ever think of.
The latest iPhone, pieces of loose paper
like important letters from the doctor or dentist.
Chewing gum for when I'm craving
and mostly expired credit cards.

Cora Newman

203 photos acting as a timeline of the last year

A message from mum – 'pick you up in ten'... she was five minutes early

Instagram with two requests. They don't get that I don't like them

The date and time (Friday 28th December, 10:52)

Reminder, 'Buy dry shampoo', dated 5th January 2013 (still haven't)

German dictionary... *Wie geht's gut*

Music from the past sixty years – skipping through songs like skipping through history

Gloucester: partly cloudy, 8°C

Calculator for when maths is approaching on the timetable

Alarm 6:54 am weekdays. I will not get out of bed until 10 am on Saturday

O2-UK

William Rooum

Rusty, jagged and sharp nails,
Several withered plants cracking through the floor,
Old stacks of books that tell tales of heroes battling
the feared and saving the innocent,
All inside a paperback book,
sad wooden toys with nothing left
but a lonesome conductor.

Katy Trivess

Fingerprints smudged on the iPad screen.
One red biro separated indefinitely from its lid.
A grubby post-it note, bent corners,
unusable.
A hardback notebook – pretty butterflies in silver and gold,
pink blossoms and the tranquillity of aqua.
Inside, infinite 'to-do' lists scrawled on each page.
It was neat once.
Loose paperclips and staples rattle together.
That long-forgotten, confiscated loomband bracelet.
Crushed Beecham's box – virus, please stay away,
you're not wanted.
A dense wad of blinding white paper, typed black print.
75 gold paper fasteners in a box.
Reminder – appointment Wednesday 8th April 2015.

Kelsey Webb

Comfy, full of fluffy feathers,
falling into a deep sleep
and a nice scent to consume.

Full of people, sweet and sour smells,
footsteps rushing around,
people stressing.

Full of flowers,
moist feelings to help them grow:
tulips, roses and daffodils,
pink, red and yellow.
Smells of dying, rotting away, losing life,
not being able to move anymore,
drifting away, browns, greys and purples.

Lilian Yeboah-Darteh

A Chinese takeaway box, decomposing lilies,
worn-out shoes, golden crucifix, the stench of rotten eggs,
letter to God, letter to Mum and Dad
and last but not least
a Bible with a verse circled:
Galatians 5:22: *But the fruit of the Spirit is love, joy, peace, patience, kindness, goodness, faithfulness.*

Poems
and Pieces of Prose

Johnathon Bishop

The Lonely Child

I am lonely in the streets.
Instead of friends
all I can hear is whistling.

No parents to secure my emotions,
no food to feed my hunger,
sharp grunts come out of my body.
Newspaper blows down the grubby streets.

Maybe if I altered my ways
I wouldn't be living this disgusting life.
As people walk past, I hear names
like *unsanitary, disgusting, disgrace to society*.

Aren't we humans too?
Just because we don't have a house, a job, or food...
I wish I wasn't treated this way.

Lion

I am a big ferocious creature
Straying stealthily into the night,
catching unaware creatures.

We are called the kings of the jungle;
we are an endangered species.
I still roar, never leaving my cubs alone.

You humans get the food for us.
I lie on the heat-sizzling rock.
Even when I sleep I protect my cubs.

I start walking through the trees –
see your cars watching me.
I growl and run away.

My School

Glass glistening on the dusty floor
as a student has broken a window.

The clock ticking on, so an hour feels like years,
a football banging on the windows at breaktime.

Tapping of the keyboards in ICT,
Hungry students waiting for the ding of break.

Students fighting outside the classroom,
banging into the door.

Teachers shouting 'Stop!'
but the students ignoring them.

Students standing up
as the front gates creak open.

Courtney Bullingham

Our School is a Zoo

We have every kind of animal
you can think of.
A zebra, a lion, a tiger, a monkey,
A flamingo, a kangaroo, and many more.
The Heart Space is where we laugh and
joke around, putting smiles on each
other's faces; we eat our lunch in there
then go outside.

We play with a ball, like the big cats
we are, chase each other like
the prey and predators we are.
Our school is a zoo,
we act like we own the school,
we act like we rule the school,
we act like we are in charge,
we scare each other but only for fun.

In reality we are normal –
you acted this way once, or it's still waiting
its turn to come around the corner and
bring your life to the crazy animal
you're meant to be.

The Snake

Sliding slowly like the sly snake I am,
I spy on my prey – that rat.
Gone in one bite.
I wrap my tail around it and watch the life drain from its eye.
I camouflage into my home,
There's no way back,
I open my eyes, see that glow until I'm gone,
I stick my teeth into your flesh,
Listen to your screams.
No one's going to hear you
In this deserted place!

My Dream Place

A clearing in the forest with a little lake which is clear blue, lily pads floating on the surface with lily flowers on top. Not a single fish or frog or tadpole. Flowers all around in different shapes and sizes and colours, like that big white and purple orchid with orange blossoms surrounding it. Big green oak trees circling the heavenly place, also known as the middle of the creepy forest. Birds chirp happily, squirrels running around in the trees and throwing their nuts to the forest floor. The smell of the fresh air and the beautiful scent of the flowers filling my nose.

My Eyes

Stare into my aquamarine eyes,
Eyes like a lake.
Swim to the deep depths.
They may not catch your attention,
but when they do you might get lost in them.
But they're short-sighted,
wear glasses with gems on the side.
My eyes: my best feature.
Do you think so too?

Louise Cronshaw

The Heart

I wonder at how such a small thing keeps us alive;
it pumps and beats, faster and faster,
it can make us cry, smile or scream.

As a child it beats,
as a teen it is all feeling,
as an adult it beats faster,
as an elder it slows down until it stops.

Trapped inside us,
beating the blood around our bodies
while we live on,
while we don't realise.

I wonder how it works.
Only scientists will know
exactly what happens within us.
Our hearts go through a lot:
love, sadness, despair.

We use The Heart as a symbol.
It doesn't look like the shape of a heart,
there must be more about it.

We never know when our last heartbeat will be:

in a second,
a minute
a day
a week
a month
a year.

Are you not scared?
One day your heart will stop
beating the blood,
stop your feelings and emotions.
Your reliable heart no longer in use.

Chloe Davis

Home

Beeping alarm clocks
Mum telling me to get out of bed
Shouting outside
Cars/vans/motorbikes revving
My brothers arguing.
Dogs barking
Things chucked on the floor.

My cosy bed.

Jealousy

You know you're not happy.
All your mates are together
and you're left alone
to fake a smile.
Jealousy says, 'Be angry. Let
them get the better of you.'
Gradually the furious monster
creeps, step-by-step, ready
to pounce.

Fireworks

Big, beautiful, sparking into the night sky,
loud bangs of glistening spark booming.
'Aren't they gorgeous?'

Anxiously waiting for the match to come alive,
giving the firework power to become a work of art,
or to injure you.

Anything can happen
in an instant…

Chelsea Dent

Pickled Onion

Not a box of heart-shaped chocolates

I give you a packet
of pickled onion crisps.

The taste of them will
stay with you as I will.

As you open them
you'll see a heart,
not a Monster Munch foot.

A crunchy heart-shaped piece of potato
fried in artificial flavouring.

Save it.

Luke Downey

Shark

I love scaring people.
It's my thing to do in my free time.
I reckon the fish swimming past are stupid
because every time they think I don't see them.
I eat them, but that's when I'm annoyed and hungry.

My jaws are like saw blades.
I'm the only horrible king of the blue sea.
I am the predator.

Winter

No warm ground

No hot sun

No ice cream van

Nice smell of veg and food

Trees waving tall and cool

Songs all about Christmas

Happy kids and adults having fun

Aaron Gomez

What Every Teenage Boy Needs

A pen, a book, an aspirin (for the headaches of school), a notebook.

A goal directed by your teachers – all fighting, wanting you to be a footballer,

a scientist, a mathematician, a writer. Your dream, nothing a teacher would expect,

an aviation engineer, building and fixing planes. A nightmare, not making it,

being a bin man who can barely stay alive, desperate to get paid.

A pen, a book, an aspirin (for the headaches of school), a notebook.

Gift

A pencil.
Normal and ordinary,
not roses, not chocolates,
but a perfect gift.

A pencil
you take everywhere,
the only one you use,
every day the pencil will sharpen –
sharpen so much people will bask in
jealousy.

Eventually that pencil will get lost
or be stolen,
but you will find another one,
a better one,
you will stick with it for years.
I am your new pencil,
I will be there
however blunt or sharp the love gets,
I'll be there.

Response to *The Broken Limber*

As the nerves build up in his body, he takes a deep breath and suits up for war. This might be his final battle. They start heading out into the battlefield that is now remembered as a graveyard. Jack, his mate and his noble steed enter the mud, but the stench of the quagmire that blocks their path strains his mind, making him want this to be just a horrible nightmare he won't wake up from until he dies. This is not the case.

As the powerful beast treads through the muck, he gets stuck. He vigorously attempts to pull his hooves out of the mud but it doesn't work. Eventually courage gets him out but he adds so much force that it also forces the pole that connects Jack with the others to break, sending his mates into certain death.

The Hand

The hand is born,
property of the child
but the hand has a dream to be
a doctor, a writer.
Life goes on and the hand is enslaved,
taken beyond its will,
and becomes a criminal,
taking items that are not its own
but come into its possession.
His master, the man, tries to take control.
He knows it's wrong but he can't stop himself.
He doesn't resist it and lets it happen.
Soon enough the man gets caught and sent to jail.
The writer asks the man what his hands have held;
he falls to the ground.
Now it's his turn,
for once...

Michal Hagner

Our Classroom

Plain grey coats hanging on coat hooks
classmates yelling at each other.
Hard, cold chairs we sit on,
dirty windows with football prints.

The Broken Limber

From the horse's point of view

We drag, we pull,
we stretch our muscles,
we roar, pulling harder
than we did before,
trying to hoist the carriage.
Splash – the mud hits our eyes,
our hardworking legs cold and numb,
slowly freezing. *Splash* – our rider falls,
the carriage sticks into the mud,
we still drag, we still pull,
we still stretch our muscles,
we still roar.

Bethany Hutton

The Valentine Door

As one door shuts another one opens…
It is stern, like our love,
It brings strength unlike a squishy teddy bear.
More opportunities will come your way.
This door shows my loyalty for us,
I would never bring you a limp rose
that would die in less than two days –
                                        I am imaginative.
The colour is a glamorous white that shines,
You can paint it with your amazing memories.
The handle is golden like your eyes
and behind it:
wedding bells, a new house, children –
                                        but those are for later…

The Struggle

BANG!
The limber broke,
leaving behind weapons
and important supplies.
Soldiers everywhere
SCREAMING,
blaming each other for the death of their allies.

Germans at gunpoint
Misery…
Dead bodies scattered
on freezing, sludgy ground,
horses treated like giant pieces of meat
as so many men were starving.

Frustration…
Soldiers cry for their wives and children,
complaining, one after the other,
as itchy, oversized uniforms cause rashes.

Terrorized sixteen year olds
Wishing they hadn't lied about their age.

As a Young Girl

Near Christmas time
I was eager to find out my presents:
a doll, a bike, makeup.
My mum shakes her head:
none of those childish things.

I retreat to the shop down the road,
stand in the cold
pressing my bare hands against the window,
stroking the reflection of the best doll in town.

Christmas morning. I run down the stairs.
A present addressed to me,
lying under the warmth of the Christmas tree.

A DOLL! The pink flesh glistening
in the blinking, broken light of my living room.

A Hundred Words of Grief

Remember the day when he took me for an adventurous journey across our town? He bought a silk dress with golden seams just for me. Shoes that were heavenly white, the nail polish as pink as Barbie – and the ring – a golden ring with big red gems gleaming in the light. That day was a surprise and overwhelming. But now... the love is no more, the ring is no more: he is no more. He has gone, without a goodbye. How selfish of him to leave everyone behind. How evil not to answer emails or calls.

Home

As I travel up the road, my eyes lock on to my house. It's weird: *house or home?* I see the tiled drive, vibrant orange bricks, a pointed porch with grey slabs beside it, glistening white windowframes, the red door with the golden number 3 slowly rusting, and the broken handle. The silver car outside which will soon be gone.
Avas Virus Update!

As I walk in I feel the warmth sticking to my body as though I were a magnet. The smell is of a floral air freshener there to impress the new guests and to disguise other scents, but further along the purple corridor I smell the radiating heat of the computer.
Avas Virus Update!

Jealousy

There it was.
The green-eyed beast
standing beside me,
not that tall but not small.
It just stood there, straight,
with fury in its eyes,
grunting at everything.
It smelled like sizzling fat.

It doesn't like people,
rarely cares what they think.
It blurts out its own ideas
to get its own way.

There it was, all jaggedy,
tasting like salt and very bitter.
Slowly it opened its mouth
and said:
'They're better than you.
They will always win.
It's not fair, it's not fair.'

Humzah Jaffer

Camouflage

This boy is serious. As he crawled through the overgrown grass he saw a helicopter taking off in the near distance. His comrades shouting, 'Get in! Get in!'

It was too late. It was gone.

Now, all alone, he was Marcus painted in dull nature colours. He was horrified as he turned round and round, having flashbacks of his family. He and his two children running in the field, laughing and jumping. Suddenly, he heard a gunshot, and he knew. As he fell to the ground a tear slid down his face. His life came to an end.

Jealousy

Flashbacks of that person having fun times.
I'm making bad prayers.
I hear his laughter,
taste burning flesh.
The fire is scorching my heart.

Bonfire Night

The rubbing of the matchstick against the matchbox.
People anxiously waiting to see the fireworks.

It sets off!

Whizzing into the sky like a bullet,
suddenly exploding, showering sparks,
illuminating the night, before it slowly disappears.

Far away, another one shoots up,
leaving a trail of green smoke,
then exploding into a pattern
of green and purple flowers.
People stand in amazement now.

The Brain

Has a mission,
a mission to become clever.
Day by day, week by week,
seeking knowledge, and overpowering
its master,
convincing him to commit trouble,
commit crimes.
From misunderstood to overpowering
the brain that controls life.

What Every Superhero Needs

A sheet of musical notes for their theme tune. Perhaps a supercar, a spare costume or a secret identity outfit. An arch nemesis; a fact file of their weaknesses and vulnerability; a freaky (but not scary) mask; a slaving sidekick. Keys to their secret HQ. A utility belt that holds sci-fi weapons. A story book of their origin, of how they became a hero.

An Empty Box

An empty box,
an unusual gift for Valentine's Day.
Why not chocolates or a diamond ring?

The empty box is my heart
ready to be filled with our laughter,
colourful eyes and your favourite drawing.

Susan Jones

The Broken Limber

Bluish-grey rain pouring from the dark, angry sky flings mud everywhere. The horses neigh fearfully, the terror clear in their eyes. The smell of death and destruction lingers in the air. The horses are pulling with all their might. The sudden loud snap of the limber echoes through the wasteland. The tired soldier pulls his numb body from his horse and, with a squelch, he lands knee-deep in black, thick mud. He heaves his legs through it and makes his way to the brown, recently abandoned cart. He pushes, but the cart stubbornly stays where it is. He thinks of leaving it, but decides against it. He needs to complete his mission. The men need these supplies and he can't let them down. He heaves the wedged cart powerfully. Suddenly the cart flies forward and the soldier lands in mud. He gets up quickly, gasping for air.

My Friend, Poppy

Venus flytrap – attractive, but deadly: if you get too close, she'll bite.

Thunder and lightning – her anger is deadly, like crashing thunder and blinding lightning. You don't want to get on her bad side.

Rainbow drops – she's sweet and unique and leaves an impression on you.

Jet black – she has her deep moments. When that happens, it's as though she travels into a world of her own where there is only darkness.

A little lane – if you mislead her she'll come crashing down, but if you lead her the right way she'll arrive at her destination.

Rocking chair – she can be old-fashioned and thoughtful. She also reminisces a lot.

Techno – she's awesome, and her tempo can change.

Raging fire – when she's angry you *will* be burnt no matter how hard you try to get away.

A cold – she's annoying sometimes, but you don't want her to go because then you'll have to go back to how you were before.

Eyelashes

The forgotten butterflies,

that hide our sapphire orbs.

Women's are tinted with chemicals,

whereas men's are under dark, bushy eyebrows.

When they fall you blow them and make a wish,

they float away from their friends,

into a world unknown.

They float down,

down,

until they land on the floor

and realise their job is done,

no longer the security guards,

that protect our sapphire orbs.

The Wolf

I am the big, bad wolf,
hunting out bunnies,
killing innocent deer.
I'm worse than a madman
with a knife.
I howl at the moon,
make you shiver with fear.
If you mess with one of us,
you mess with us all.
You wouldn't want to be there
when I come to call.
When blood is shed
you know I'm near.
I am your worst fear.

School

The eerie sound of heavy breathing.
The teacher's annoyed look
when her class won't settle.
Tension in the air
as two students glare at each other.
Dim lights flickering on and off.
A romantic movie blaring next door,
so girls swoon and boys sneer.
The sweet aroma of the teacher's perfume
making a few people gag.
The awkward silence that follows
after a teacher makes a joke.
Ink dripping from a broken biro.

Vikki Kirby

There Used to Be Five…

One became sad and then they became four
because One wasn't happy anymore.
A summer's day on the beach,
a lonely day on the cliffs just didn't end well.
One was depressed, on the edge,
watching the other four party and play.
Wishing, just wishing she could have another day.
Did it have to be One's last day?
Why couldn't she party and play?
'I'm a coward,' One thought,
as the moments dragged by.
All she could think of was sleepovers with five.
Those happy moments.

Feet

Right foot, you let me down;
grew from a size three to a size six
almost overnight.

Now you hurt when I run
and will never be strong enough
for what I wanted you to be.

You were happy in that small shoe,
good at athletics.
My size sixes are not,

growing more painful
as I use them.
My bones rub on my tendons.

No one can see these things.
They are there and extremely frustrating.
I will never be part of Team GB.

I keep you confined in a pair of cute socks
so people can't see the monsters inside.
Nail varnish makes no difference.

I wish I had feet sandals would love
instead of these; bony and strange at the heel.
A mirror image of my dad's.

Feet – you let me down.

Poppy Limbrick

My Friend, Susan

is a lily,
hailstones in May,
an Easter egg – she can get broken when something hits her.
She is dark purple,
a little sail boat,
a sponge as she takes opinions in, then when she absorbs too
much, just bursts out in anger.
She is classical music
and water.

Hair

A curtain that hides me from the world.
Falling streaks of brown
almost touching the ground,
like a dark Rapunzel
if I let down my hair.
When the wind comes it makes a cape behind me.
Always in a mess,
has a mind of its own.
Just dyed but the colour unnoticed.
Sadly the colour will fade away.
Goodbye brown hair – you will start turning grey.

My hair is what makes me unique,
and even if my hair and I have differences,
my hair is my friend.

Kyania May

Wolf

I'm the big, bad wolf.
I search the mountains,
looking for my next victim.
Watch as I howl for my pack.
Razor claws, we tear apart our well-deserved meal.
Crunch, crunch – we even devour the bones.
We spread back out to cover our area.
We don't like trespassers.
Grey and white, that's our colour.
You'd better watch out.
Our savage, gold eyes are on patrol.

What Every Teenage Girl Should Carry

My boyfriend gave me a diamond ring.
I added my makeup bag, hand sanitiser,
a couple of packs of chewing gum, earphones,
a year-old love letter and some hairpins.
I have a lucky charm.
There is room for my guilt – those secrets and lies. Bangles.
A lock. Fury from jealous girls that talk behind my back.
    Perfume.
A pink purse. His smile, his kindness, my happiness.
That wonderful humour, my love.
Tissues, just in case.

Valentine Present

I give you this apple.
Not heart-shaped chocolates.
Its beautiful, red wrapping paper protects
The sweet but sour goodness inside.
It's brimming with hope for the future
And will bring you good health.
Have it.
The tenderness will make you feel at ease.
It hides more gifts in its core.
Not red roses, nor balloons that say 'I love you' –
I give you this russet apple.

The House

Small compact,
dark and silent with no one around,
I feel that I'm being watched.
Three squeaky steps that creak on their own,
two messy bedrooms that looks like a bomb's gone off
and a lockable bathroom that gives me the chills.
Black and red wallpaper that peels easily.
In the corners of the room thick, dust-covered webs
cling onto the ceiling.
The musty smell comes from the mould-covered window.
Dirt and dust clumped together, sticking to all surfaces they
    can find.
Even animals would stay away
if they could see what lies in this house.

The Masked Woman

Day after day, the woman sits on the same bench, staring into space. No one knows who she is or where she is from. People try to avoid her, but their curiosity is too strong. They sit down beside her and say a cheerful, 'Hello' or 'Good morning'. She turns her head slightly and glares into their eyes, saying nothing. She never leaves home without her mask. The mask stares people in their eyes and never loses. It's as if it's a part of her and is keeping her prisoner in her own mind.

She is the masked woman.

Hands

Tiny, delicate hands with perfectly shaped nails
reach out,
grip pens, hold spoons, quickly getting used to
their surroundings.
In time these little hands grow,
their nails short and jagged or painted pretty patterns,
fingers lengthen, palms expand,
working non-stop, all day: writing,
picking things up, typing.
Holding another hand – they start
to understand love.
These hands reach out.

Cora Newman

The Brain

Controls my everything,
making my every move.
I trust it with my life –
I don't know it all, you know.
It learns,
taking information through my
eyes,
ears,
mouth,
nose,
fingers,
capturing that perfect moment through the lens of my eyes like a camera,
listening to that one song I know every single line to as if I were born knowing.
The taste of cheese pizza melting in my mouth,
smelling the boy's scent on his jumper, given to me as I'm collapsing in the cold air,
the touch of my keypad on my phone – soft and flat.
Jellyfish do not have a brain… But you do.

Hatred

boils up inside,
is a spiky bed of nails that no one wants to smooth out,
makes my nose burn.
It is red and scorching, coming towards me,
creeping up behind, ready to pounce,
smelling like mouldy bread stuck
in the bottom of the bin that no one wants to face.
It tastes like hot, spicy food that starts a fire in my belly,
sneaks up and whispers into my ear…
'What's your problem?'

#Hate
Definition
boils up inside, jumps out like a jack-in-the-box.

Hair

Brush your greased hair, strand by strand.
Slick it back into a ponytail.
Pull tight.
Give yourself only fifty per cent of your circulation.
Place the £1.50 spongey, wired doughnut
through your ponytail.
Spread the excess hair around the doughnut.
Tuck in your split ends so they can't be seen.
Pierce a couple of bobby pins through the gaps
of your hair.
Admire from each angle.
Plod along to school.

My Hundred Word Story?

I can't do it. I just can't. I've tried and tried, over and over, but I just can't. The mounds of paper tower around me – Staples would be proud! I keep thinking, but not one brain cell can help me. I'm considering rehab. Letters are appearing on the paper but make no words. Not even Shakespeare can help me out now. I tear up pages and pages of pointless scribbles and get no closer to what I need.

BUT WAIT!

Through all of my moaning and groaning, I seem to have found what I finally need. My hundred words.

Whale

I give you this whale as a token of my affection,
it may get in the way sometimes,
like me,
but you'll love it in the end.
The bristles drag you in,
his noise is as of love pounding
through the sound waves, into your ears.
His captivating size is as big as your heart filling up with love.

So this may not be a teddy bear holding his heart in his hands
for you,
or a fancy box of chocolates,
but it is a whale… and it whaley loves you,
as do I.

Scarlet Organ

LOVE

Love is powerful, it conquers all.
Love can be from friends or family.
Love is passion and soul.
You may love a little or a lot.
Love is one of the things you cannot hide.

LIFE

Life is given to all, sometimes taken away.
Life can be taken for granted or cherished for years.
Life can be long or short.
Life is what you make of it.

Jessica Perry

Nut

This will be short, and it will be sweet.

I give you a nut.
It's hard on the outside and on the inside.
You have to try your hardest to crack it.
You might not succeed, but try.

I will be a challenge –
I'm a tough almond, you see.
I knew you wouldn't expect this.
I'm surprised you haven't run away.

My Eyes

I used to have so-called 'perfect' eyesight;
kids at my school never wore glasses.
Then I was in class looking at the board
and the writing was blurred, unfocused.
I couldn't see anything far away.

I thought I was special.
Swimming became a struggle.
People made fun of my glasses,
called me *four* eyes.
I hated wearing them.
I'd had enough.

Now everyone is wearing glasses!

William Rooum

December

No hot summer breeze,
but the icy winter wind,
no smell of sizzling sausage,
but the warm smell of roasting chestnuts,
no splashing of pools with children playing,
but the screeching of children slipping over in an ice rink,
no cheap summer inflatables,
but the laughs of children constructing a makeshift sled,
no green crisp grass,
but the white mask that covers the field.

An Arm

I will give you nothing, except an arm.
Yes, an arm.
A limb that could be broken and mended.
A muscly arm to carry you.
Muscles covered by skin
you can touch.
Goose-pimpled when I see you,
Each hair a standing ovation.

Fly

I'm an annoying bugger.
I'm the buzz at the bin.
I follow you for your ice cream.
We don't die out too fast for prey,
always buzzing,
on the hunt for rotting food.
We can fit through any hole,
hunt as a swarm.
We annoy you at every second,
living off scraps from the ground.
We are a pain in the arse
up to the point of you surrendering your food.

Conor Strutt

The Lonely House

I am the lonely house,
Alone on this lonely street.
Empty and dusty inside; filled with bugs.

Bugs are my only friends,
crawling all over my insides,
giving me coughs and sickness.
Bugs catch the flies buzzing around.

The hairy flies tickle my throat and there's nothing I can do.
The sick-eating flies leave dead bodies in my empty body
and in their sticky cobwebs.
The egg-laying flies fill the gaps inside me
with their gooiest eggs; I feel violated.

I am the lonely house. I only want someone to care,
but there's no one there.

The Broken Limber

The ground was deep, sticky mud.
It smelled horrid – dead bodies covered the ground;
it made me feel sick.
The horses screamed in fear
as explosions went off all around us.
Suddenly, the limber snapped and the horses let out
a loud roar as they felt the pain from the broken cart's limber.
My fingers were numb. It was so cold.

Kelsey Webb

Broken Record

Listening to love songs
Just days before Valentine's

Notice
I give you a record
Not any old record
A broken record
Chipped, scratched and scarred
But still precious.

Sorry
Not roses, teddies or chocolates

But the rhythm of slow songs
Old classics
No difference
It will give you passion and thought
I give you a record, the touch a bass
The touch sharp, rough and uneven

I hope this present
Stands up to your expectations
Even though not a diamond solitaire

Not as strong as a kiss
No depth
Not my emotion
Just this.

The Broken Limber

An ordinary day going into battle...

It's 0600 and the Germans open fire on us. My horses just came out from the dark stables. We are stuck inside this sludgy, gooey mud, hoping we will get out. I'm anxious – I don't know what to do, trying my hardest to get feeling. My hands are burning and rubbing against the ropes, so I smell blistering skin. I am still stressed, hearing my horses screaming and galloping their fastest to get out of this nightmare.

I can tell that my horses are struggling, trying to drag themselves out of the mud, neighing, getting shot.

I smell the terrible stench of mud and horse manure, smell my own sweat coming off my clothes, dripping down my forehead into my eyes.

The packages are falling off the carriage. I try to save them all but at the same time try to make the horses ready. I feel cold on the back of my neck, but my fingers are so numb I can't feel them.

My mouth is dry and mud is splattering onto my lips. I rub them with my cold jumper, which is itching. My boots are hurting me; they keep on falling off. I'm trying to struggle them back on, lice and fleas crawling down my legs, hanging onto my leg hairs. That isn't the end of my problems.

This has happened before. This is happening all the time in this war; I don't think anything is going to get me through. I think this is the end. I think I am going to die.

That Inside Feeling

The pipe on the ceiling with its plain grey colour, drooping, looks as though it's going to fall. Plain white wall, scratch marks on the places that have no colour. The scary mask on the back of the colourful wall makes the room feel frightening. The work with horrific images adds tension. Loud students jump on tables and chairs, pencils thrown around the room from one side to another like it's a tennis court. The texture and roughness on my chair with the hard backing, so when I lean back it hurts. A disgusting perfume or deodorant, which feels like it's burning my nose. No sun comes through the windows, just loud dripping noises from the rain, like banging drums – with that inside feeling that the rain will come through.

Lilian Yeboah-Darteh

Fireworks

The embracing warmth of my own room as I sit on the uncomfortable chair getting ready to watch the show made for the sky. What would it smell like? Will I sit or stand while I watch it outside? Will my friends shriek and holler? Or will I sit there in wonder at the faded bangs and fizzes?

Finally, the first firework shoots up and the opening act begins. The golden white flower of the sky illuminates.

That

That person's coat is hooked up like the ones I used to see,
the murky purple wall, the charts that show their name but
never mine,
the fairy lights that watch me from behind,
sunshine that blinds my eye
the sweet smells of jasmine and candyfloss burn my nose,
that blue piece of rubber that numbs my butt,
the annoying buzzing that never stops, and that constant
breathing of that person.

I Give You a Lemon

Not the sweetness of chocolate,
but the sour sting of a lemon.
It is a zest for life.
It is a piece of sunshine,
like the bright smiles of love.

It will bring you to pout,
ready for that sour kiss.
It will make your mouth tingle with bliss.

I give you a lemon.

Royalty

I'm too beautiful for you.
I am the colours of the rainbow.
I have a trail of yellow dust.
I'm a fragile being.
Too delicate for your hands to hold.
I am admired by all creatures, irresistible.
We are the royalty of the insect world.

Hatred

Hatred has no face,
stays at the back in the dark
waiting to pounce,
its stench so foul your nose burns.

Each step it takes, it starts to form
a familiar face; family or friend.

No one is safe from hatred.
The silhouette breathes heavily,
forming slow words, choking you,
filling with doubts and needs.

Have you ever been captured
by hatred? Trapped by his words?

Hatred will takes us down,
one by one.

Resolution

When the New Year came I made a promising start, with a promise to go with it:

I, Lilian Yeboah-Darteh, shall be the first person to ride a kangaroo in China.
I shall rewrite history with my own hands,
I shall mock the ones who mocked me,
I shall laugh in your faces and spit on it,
because when I laugh I spit – but, anyway, I shall go on with the year.

When the New Year came I made a promising start, with a promise to go with it:

I, Lilian Yeboah-Darteh, will learn how to cut shapes.

Home Is…

The forbidden cat that lives below our flat.
The lamppost light that just won't go off.
The sound of your mum praying, and the praises of songs.
The beating sound of drums and trumpets call…
What is home?

A restricted place of religion and etiquette.
The stern voices that quarrel secretly.
The salty tears that fall with grief and plea.

Religion is a cage that shrinks in time.
Age is a number that grows in a lifetime.

Home is…

The forbidden cat that lives below our flat.
The lamppost light that just won't go off.
The sound of your mum praying, and the praises of songs.
The beating sound of drums and trumpets call…
What is home?

Dinner

Dinner was served. That sludge called soup was going to be more interesting than they thought. That ordinary day – or so they thought – was turning out for the worse. An undescribed person, whatever you may call them, was coming.

When that knock resounded, it almost shook the house with intent to strike fear, but what did they know? Nothing. Sometimes it is better to know nothing than know all.

What a coincidence that the door was left open by a small, intrigued girl. One step and the man's stern face deepened, if that was even possible. The stage was set for a downfall, nothing of which anyone, not even this mysterious guest, knew of. *BANG!* He knelt down. An act of repentance? Long, dark hair hid his face. 'Forgive me.' His voice was a harsh whisper as though he had been shouting.

'Who are you? What are you talking about?' said the girl.

'Forgive me, forgive me, please, I beg of you!' the mystery man kept repeating.

The young girl realised how tense he was. She stepped back, worried about what this man wanted.

The normal banter that filled the family table seemed to have been replaced by a tension that felt unnerving. Eating became unbearable despite the hunger that resided at the back of their dry throats.

About the Writers

Johnathon Bishop

I am sixteen years old. My hobbies are gaming and watching TV. The kind of games I enjoy are *Call of Duty*, *Grand Theft Auto* and *Halo* because they are so realistic. I currently live with my mother and sister. My plan for when I leave Gloucester Academy is to go to college to do a computing course. I would like to come back to Gloucester Academy and work as an information and communication technologies technician because I have been interested in computers since I was six years old.

Courtney Bullingham

My name is Courtney Jane Bullingham and I am fourteen years old. I write because it's a way I can release my feelings and thoughts without giving too much away. I don't really tell people how I feel because I think they can feel what I feel through my writing. I don't only write poems and stories – I write songs as well. My inspiration was probably my best friend Susan as she introduced me to the First Story club, and she proved I don't need to keep my feelings bottled up. Oh, and my English teacher, because she gives me ideas and pushes me to work my hardest.

Me by Courtney

Sweet and sour chicken,
raging storm,
a really tight ring that turns your finger blue,
downy, curly hair,
a lion,
an open and chewing mouth,
Monopoly,
I am neon pink!

Louise Cronshaw

I'm a fourteen-year-old girl, Louise Sally Cronshaw, born on September 23rd 2000 and lived for a while in Manchester. I moved to Spain with my mum and brother, lived there for eight years, moved to Manchester, then to Gloucester. I am fluent in Spanish. I have been a writer since I started Year 9. My favourite writers: David Walliams and JK Rowling. My aspirations in life are to go to sixth form, then university in London to study fashion design. I would like to work with celebrities in places all around the world.

Me! by Louise

Pizza
Sun flower   Crazy driver
Pop   Moon
Four-person leather chair
Summer
Pair of pink odd socks
Fake dyed blonde long hair
Panda bear
Mouth   Jenga
Fuchsia pink

Chloe Davis

English is my favourite subject, and writing is something I like to do a lot, but I dislike reading. My phone is my best friend and I can't manage without the internet. I have always lived in Gloucester with my mum, dad and two brothers.

Chelsea Dent

I like to write. My favourite thing to write about is life, as we all have one. If you didn't know me you would think I am a quiet girl – but you would be wrong as I am a crazy girl with purple hair, and I also want the ends of my hair dip-dyed blue as it's my favourite colour. My writing inspiration is when I am on my Facebook and I see a post and I get inspired to write a new quote about life: for example, my favourite is *live the life you want to live not the life others want you to live*.

Me by Chelsea

I am fish, not everyone likes me
I am like Gloucestershire weather as I can be all happy
then just flip and be mad for no reason
I think of myself as a pineapple as I can be horrible on the outside
but the inside of me can be nice and caring
I am the colour white as you never know exactly how I feel
I am a cat as I can be vicious but also kind at the same time
I am a bed as it can be comfortable but also hard to sleep on

Luke Downey

I am twelve years old and I am in Year 8. I live with my nan and my brother. My hobbies are playing *Call of Duty* and *Halo*. I like *Halo* because it's got a brilliant storyline but *Call of Duty* has the most action. I support Manchester United.

Aaron Gomez

My name is Aaron Gomez. I'm twelve years of age. My inspiration for writing is from games. I play many games so I see a variety of designs and lots of imaginative ideas – and when I come to write a story I can use all of them in one, which makes for a great story! Originally I wanted to be an aviation engineer when I leave school, but I might pursue a career as a graphic designer instead, as when I started to stay after school to do photography we worked with Photoshop and I really enjoyed it. If I could, I would spend all my time doing Photoshop.

Me by Aaron

I am the KFC that makes people's day.
I am the sunshine that can turn to thunder real quick.
I am the gym sharks that are too big for you but you still want to use them.
I am a clean cut with a mistake.
I am a lion with the brain of a cub.
I am a mouth. I am Monopoly.
I am yellow with a shade of red.

Michal Hagner

I was born in Poland on 26th January 2002. I came to England when I was seven and I still speak Polish. I live with my Mam, Dad, two sisters and one brother. My favourite colour is bright green, because it reminds me of happiness. I like reading psychological thrillers. My favourite is *The Bunker Diary* by Kevin Brooks. I am a slow reader, but it does not bother me. When I grow up I want to be a cook or a chef, because I love cooking! My hobbies are drawing, cooking, reading, watching movies and learning.

Bethany Hutton

My name is Bethany Grace Hutton. I was born in 2001 on the 4th of May or International Star Wars Day, which explains why I like Star Wars. I AM NOT A NERD! I am a weirdo though. I love photography. I am the crafty type. 'Arty farty', as my mum always says. In my opinion technology is ruining the world but without it you wouldn't be reading this. I am a very loud and sarcastic person who is very open. Today is my whatever day so today I have a lot of crazy weird and wonderful thoughts. I am a simple person with a lot of opinions and I think I'm always right, unless physically proven wrong.

Me by Bethany

A red Haribo loveheart, as I am squishy and made of sugar and spice and everything nice, and I'm very sweet to people I like
An advertisement theme tune for *CBeebies* as I can be quiet and hyper all at the same time
I am a rash as I'm always there, and hang around for longer than expected
I am OBVIOUSLY Trivial Pursuit as I wind people up, and I know all the answers.
I am the misty greyish-blue that wisps up just before a storm
I am a hyperactive koala as I cling on to things I want, look cute and fluffy but can be feisty
I am a slight shower as I am annoying and graceful at the same time plus I spread my weirdness little drops at a time

Humzah Jaffer

I am thirteen years old. I am a Muslim and I was born on the 1st of October 2001. Every day I see new things, which makes me imagine what my future job will be. An engineer, or an author that writes books? I hate books and writing stories, even if it is fiction or non-fiction, but if I keep writing I enjoy it because my imagination is shown. I mostly get my imagination from movies such as action/horrors, and I do play computer games which I enjoy.

Me by Humzah

I am the parrot you can't get enough of,
the thunder that stays quiet,
the cap that doesn't fit.
A curly, huge afro which is too much to carry,
a shark that cannot swim,
a mouth that likes to speak but is shy.
Monopoly that drives you crazy and annoyed,
I am blue tinged with a light shade of grey.

Susan Jones

I was born on the 11th of September 2001. I have an older step-sister whom I've never met and a little sister who is eight years old. My mum is very weird but I love her anyway. My dad died when I was six. Even though I can't really remember him, I still miss him, which might sound weird but it's the truth. My dream for the future is to be a Japanese-to-English translator and a Spanish-to-English translator. I'm going to have to work hard and try my best, which is why I intend to go to college then university. My inspiration comes from my friends who tell me secrets and those secrets inspire me for some reason.

Me! by Susan

A spicy pepperoni pizza,
raging hail, handbag,
a Japanese bob,
protective wolf,
eyes, chess,
dark red.

Vikki Kirby

Victoria Kirby, Female, 14
Important People: Dad (Russell Kirby), Mum (Georgina Kirby), Chummy (Louise Cronshaw) and many others but we only had 200 words.

Background: Parents separated, two homes, two families, two lives.

Favourite writer: Cathy Glass

Emotions: Anger and happiness, but I keep myself to myself and there's a lot that people don't know about me – I like it that way.

Hobbies: Sporty athlete (hammer throw, 1500m)

Current Favourite songs: Panic! at the Disco's 'I Write Sins Not Tragedies' and Ed Sheeran's 'Afire Love'.

Job ambitions: Army nurse. I'm in Year 9, looking ahead for the future, and I'm into science. If I have an opinion I'll say how it is.

Me by Vikki

Watermelon
Daisies
Golf buggy
Street dance
Sun
Comfy old chair
Winter
Running longs
Plain ponytail
Lamb
Dark eyes
Monopoly
Purple

Poppy Limbrick

I am thirteen and I am in Year 8. I have four amazing brothers but I only live with one and I live with my mum and my dad. I'm usually on Xbox most of the day. I used to play games nonstop, then I hardly got invited to play so now I am usually on YouTube, blasting my favourite songs, blocking the world out. I also love to watch anime and read manga. My top three favourite animes are *Vampire Knight*, *Another* and *Black Butler*. My favourite manga is *Mamotte! Lollipop* (*Save Me! Lollipop*) which only took me a day to read and so I started reading it over again. Then, when I lost the books, I watched the anime and the whole anime/manga just makes me laugh and cry as I feel for the characters.

Me by Poppy

Ice cream, snow, a bracelet
Simple hairstyle, panda bear, ears
Snakes and ladders, a mix of colours.

Kyania May

I am thirteen years old. My inspiration for writing poems is often from books that I've read, but I don't have a favourite author because I like reading different types of books. I also get my inspiration from movies and TV drama that I watched or really liked. The best environment for me when I'm writing is being alone because then I can get more done and I can be more creative. My everyday life is normal: I live with my mum and her boyfriend and my dog Elley who I love lots. My dad lives in Northampton with my sister and the rest of my brothers. I do have one brother that lives in Gloucester, but he's a troublemaker. I love listening to music. My favourite genre is pop but I always listen to Nicki Minaj because she's amazing and is really good at singing and rapping. I hope I can carry on writing poems and stories that other people will enjoy.

Me! by Kyania

I'm a warm and freshly baked cheesy pizza,
topped with pepperoni that makes your day.
I'm a blizzard of snow that could last for hours.
An old worn-out pair of Nike trainers.
Long, golden ringlets as perfect as a china doll's.
A leopard.
A foot.
I'm the Game of Life.
I am crimson red.

Cora Newman

I am full of sarcasm and wit, which I drown my writing in. I don't think about what I write; I just think about what I find amusing and, as I don't like reading, I think about the kind of book people like me will not put down – and hopefully I'm doing alright. My influence is myself. I do what I want and I let people judge because it gives them something to do. I don't have to tell you what I'm like because I think you can work it out.

Me by Cora

Japanese pink blossom tree
Earth, a recliner
Spring, tutu
Long ringlets, baby turtle
Double chin, Scrabble
Emerald green
Learner driver, 50s jive.

Scarlet Organ

My name is Scarlet Lynsie-Jane Organ. I am fourteen years old, born December 1st 2000.

I have eight sisters and three brothers between my parents who have each been married twice. I am an introvert and like being away from large crowds. Ever since I was a little girl I have always enjoyed reading, writing, drawing, photography and listening to music. My favourite colours are black, red, blue and purple. My favourite author is Michael Morpurgo because I find his bookings very interesting and calming but also very emotional. One of my favourite things to do is watch films that have been made from a book and seeing which is better. I believe that anyone can be inspired to be an author because there is so much to write about around the world, and so many opportunities.

Me by Scarlet

Spicy Texas Chicken Wings
a tornado
black ripped jeans/red high heels
dark purple messy fishtail plait
King Cobra Snake
a jaw
Blackjack

Jessica Perry

I was born on June 1st 2001 – that makes me a Gemini, so I am very two-faced and have a mixed personality, which some people may not like. My favourite colours are black & white (basically monochrome). I live with my single mum, who raised my sister and me up all by herself. I have always wanted to be a VET!

William Rooum

I like sarcasm and rugby. I smell nice. I'm not one of those who sits still and quiet, though I like books. My favourite author is Michael Morpurgo, and my favourite novel of his is *Running Wild*, the one about the elephant. I've enjoyed expressing my feelings through this course as I'm the class clown and don't get to do it often. My writing is more serious than I seem in real life.

Conor Strutt

I'm sixteen years old and a Year 11 student at Gloucester Academy. I go to tae kwon do, which I've been doing for nearly nine years. I like to play on my Xbox and I like to play games like action and adventure. I also do cadets every week (apart from the holidays). When I leave school I want to become an electrician. I have enjoyed being a part of First Story because it has allowed me to experience something different.

Katy Trivess

I have been a teacher of English at Gloucester Academy since January 2014. I love to read and it has been lovely to write for pleasure during the First Story sessions and a privilege to be a part of First Story, working alongside Cheltenham Festivals. Our writer-in-residence, Alicia Stubbersfield, has been an inspiration to our students who have grown in confidence and produced such poignant writing. I enjoyed taking students to the First Story Festival at Lady Margaret Hall, Oxford, where they bought books and had them signed by writers such as Mark Haddon and James Dawson. This anthology, with a front cover created by art students at the University of Gloucestershire, will be something to treasure forever.

Me by Katy

A ham salad sandwich, made with love.
Hot, shimmering sunshine through silver clouds.
A cosy dressing gown.
Golden blonde hair, loose curls on a special day.
A cautious soft kitten.
Vacant, azure, tired eyes.
The Game of Life.
Moody blue.

Kelsey Webb

My name is Kelsey Jade Webb. I was born on 5th October 2000, that's why I never forget my age. I love to do art, mainly portraits, My mum is always praising me because of it. I love action films and sci-fi brings out the nerdy side of me. I enjoy writing short stories, mainly about romantic objects. I also love to do illustrations. My inspiration to write is my drawings, to write about them and what they mean to me.

Me by Kelsey

Marmite on toast.
Barbie theme tune.
A bad case of the flu.
Monopoly millionaire.
Fiery red.
Dolphin.
Hail.
Black and white beanie.

Lilian Yeboah-Darteh

My name is Lilian with a very long surname. I'm a girl in a very odd way. I've been a writer for twenty weeks I would say. My inspiration is the will to find the meaning of life and the future for me and my friends. I'm a black African with the ambition to see the world in a way no one has seen before, for my name to go down in history. I know it may be too big for a girl like me but once you have your priorities straight you can do anything you want to do.

Me by Lilian

There is a girl,
not a fanatic boy who loves to play football.

A girl.
She has something: a talent – or a nuisance,
others may say.

Her name is Lilian.
She is loud.

She can't juggle balls or ride a unicycle
and no, she isn't great at sport, either.
Somehow she manages to make others laugh.

And to her, it's something to hold on to,
something to help her on her life's journey.
That one thing could be her chance
to make herself known to others.

Her laugh is contagious,
her smile is bright.

Laughter is a drug,
something that can cure us
of sadness and loneliness.